Flannel Kisses

Linda Crotta Brennan received a Masters in Early Childhood Education from Rhode Island College and is a full-time writer and instructor with the Institute of Children's Literature.
Ms. Brennan lives in Coventry, Rhode Island with her husband and three daughters.

Mari Takabayashi was born in Tokyo, Japan and studied at Otsuma Women's College. She moved to New York in 1990, where she lives with her husband and their daughter.
Ms. Takabayashi is also the illustrator of *Rush Hour* by Christine Loomis.

Flannel Kisses

Linda Crotta Brennan
Illustrated by Mari Takabayashi

A Division of The **McGraw·Hill** Companies

www.sra4kids.com

SRA/McGraw-Hill

*A Division of The **McGraw·Hill** Companies*

Send all inquiries to:
SRA/McGraw-Hill
8787 Orion Place
Columbus, OH 43240-4027

Printed in the United States of America.

ISBN 0-07-572227-5

3 4 5 6 7 8 9 QST 06 05 04 03

For my husband, who warms me with his flannel kisses.
—L.C.B.

For my husband, Kam, and our daughter, Luca.
—M.T.

Flannel sheets,
Cold floor,

Hot oatmeal,

Out the door!

Slippery snowsuit,
Sticky snow,

Pack a snowball,

Make it grow.

Pile snowballs,

Small on fat.

Crown icy head
With fuzzy hat.

Dry socks,
Soup's best.

Red nose rubs

Dad's flannel chest.

Back outside,

Dig snowy square,

Stove and table,
Hard-packed chair.

Toes cold,
Cheeks red,

Smell hot stew,

Baking bread.

Fireside story,

Say good night,

Flannel kisses
By pale starlight.